"The Little Red R

Written and Illustrated by
Shane Williams

a little red robot.

He lived in a

Surrounded by

Some were big and fierce looking,

But there was one animal who had no friends. He was alone.

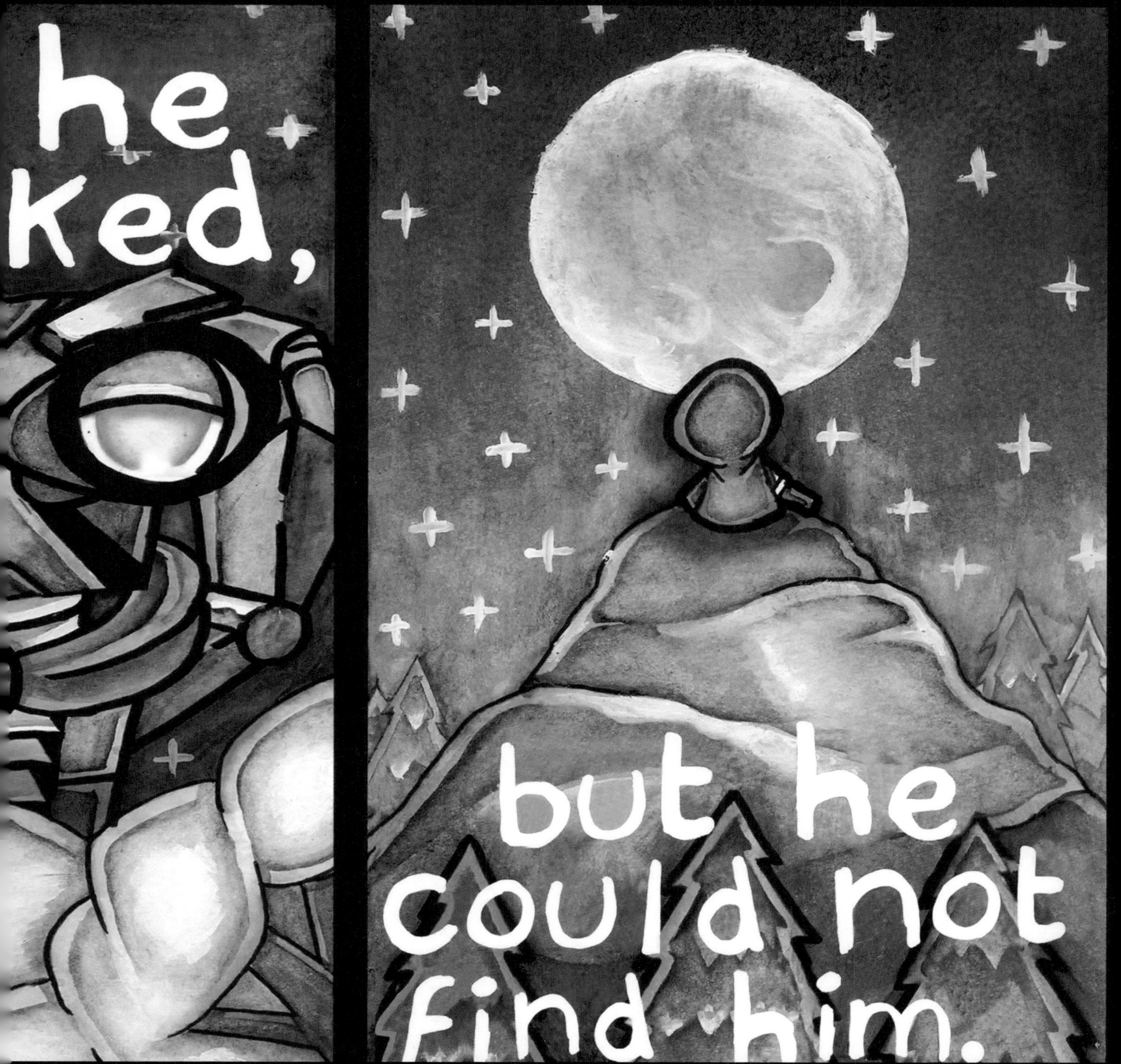
he
ked,
but he
could not
find him.

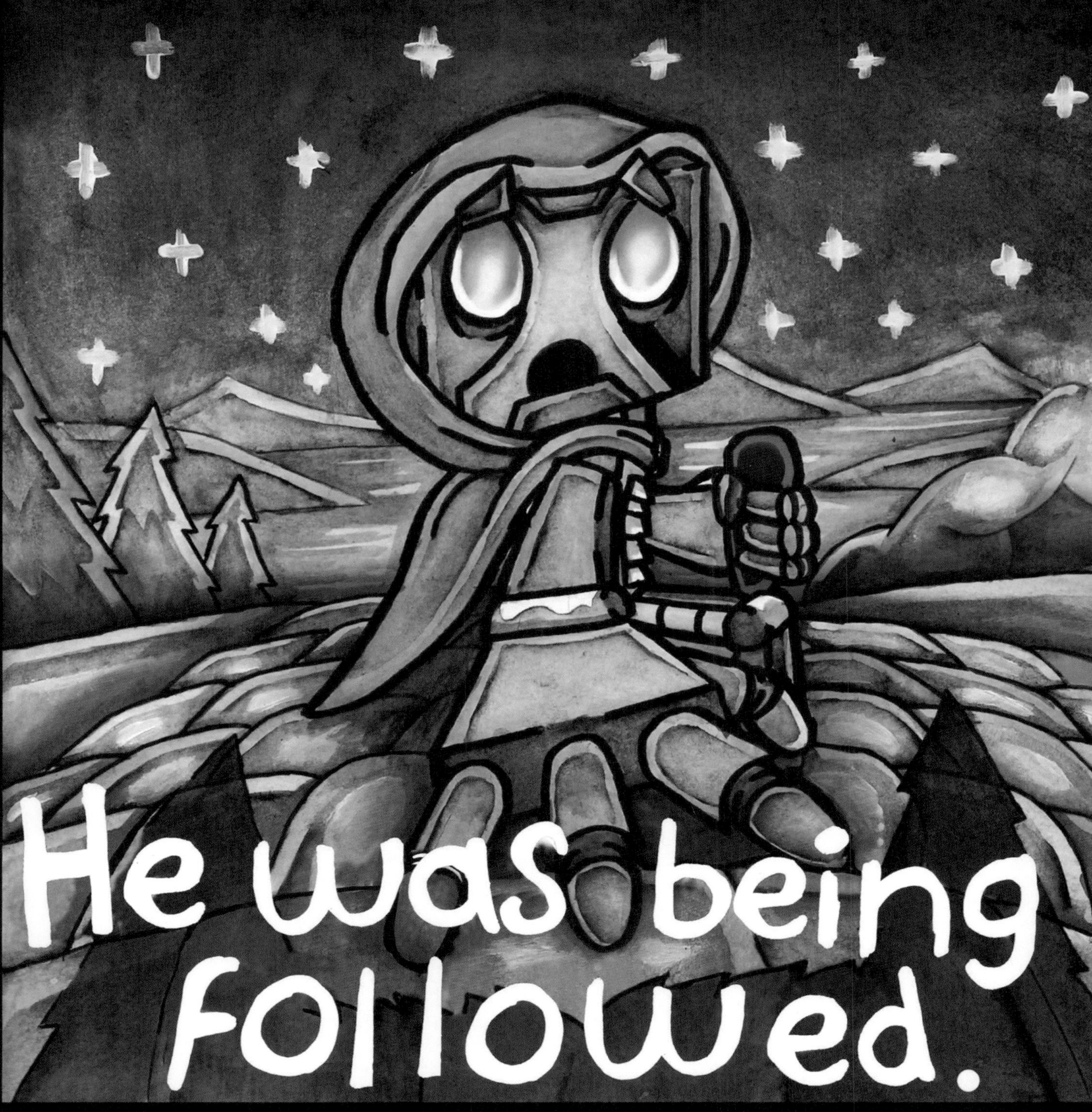
He was being
followed.

Behind him was the animal that was all alone. A big wolf!

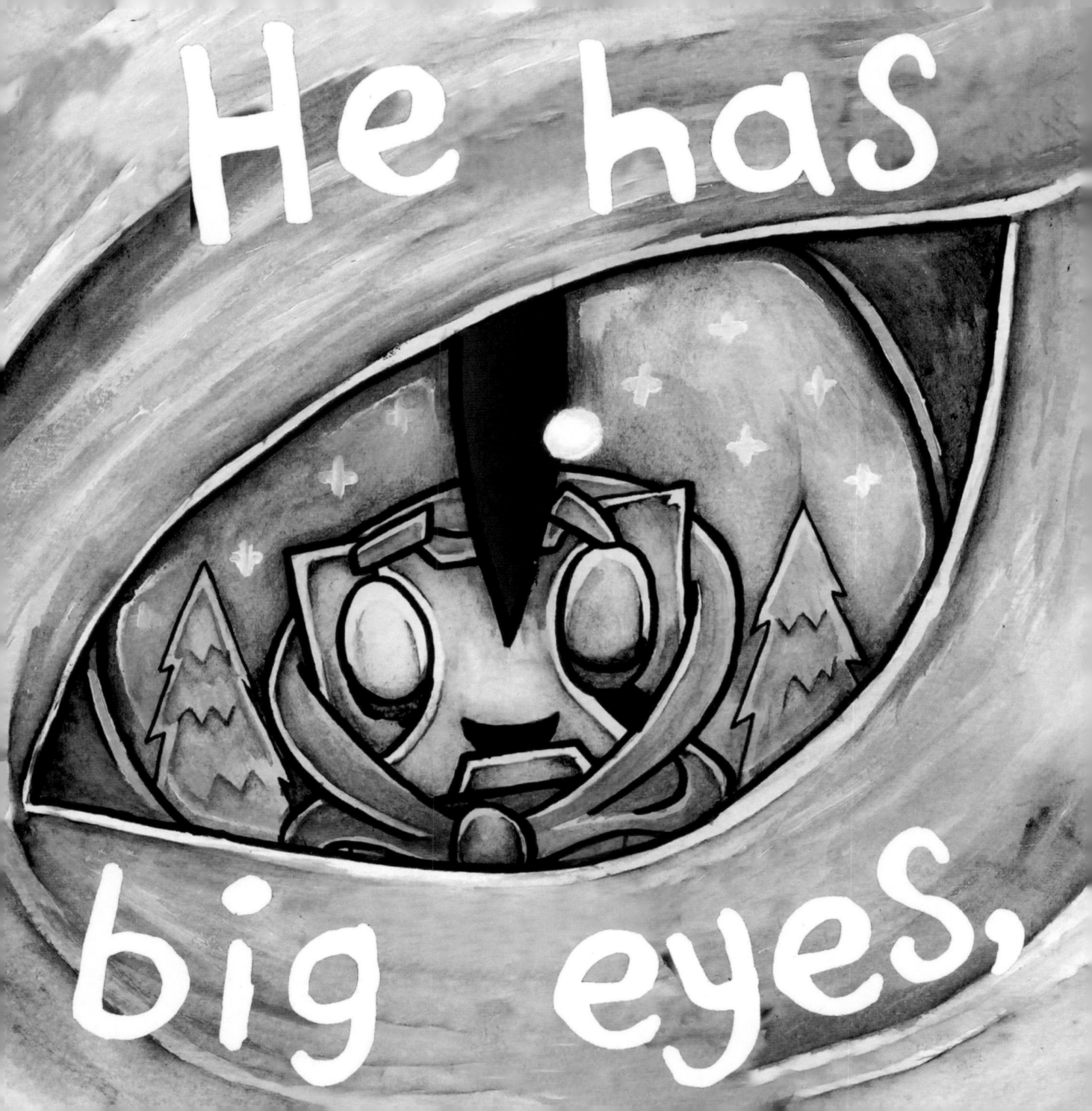
He has
big eyes,

The Wolf looked Suprised. "You don't fear me? No one wants to be my friend", he replied Sadly.

The Little robot smiled, "I don't fear you. I am sad that you are alone"

"I will be your friend!"

They spent the night watching the stars,

and both grew to like one another.

the sun rose they went everywhere together. Wolf and the little red robot became the best of friends.

The End

My name is Shane Williams, and I'm a freelance
Illustrator who mainly works in watercolour.
As well as watercolour I create art with
digital. pencil and mixed media.
I live in the Uk and I've done art since I was a kid,
being brought up with Marvel and Dc comics.
I graduated from Wolverhampton University,
completing a BaHons Degree in Illustration with a 2.1.
I hope you enjoy my story and please, don't hesitate in
contacting me.

Contact:

www.Scwillustrations.com

Instagram: Scwillustrations

Phoenix.risen@Hotmail.com

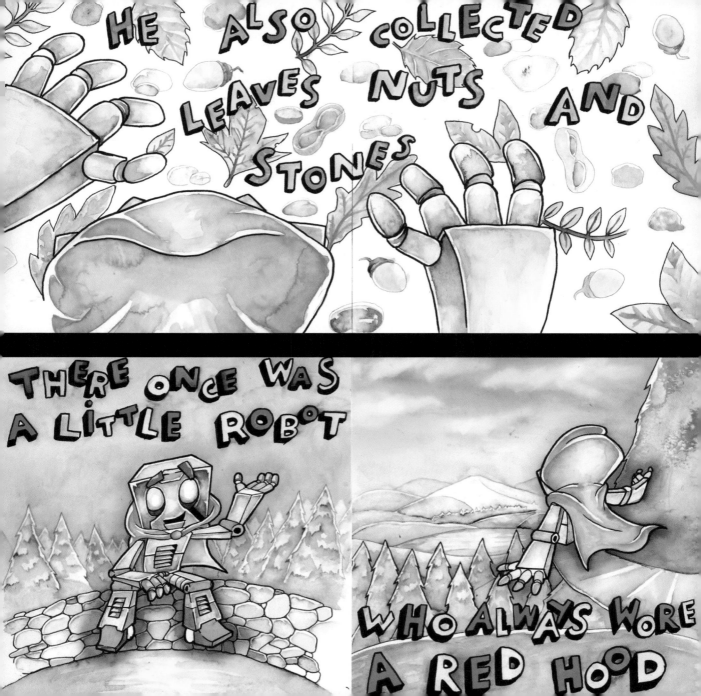

Printed in Poland
by Amazon Fulfillment
Poland Sp. z o.o., Wrocław